"Good Job Bringing That Plane In, Young Man," Said the Surgeon. "It Looks to Be Pretty Badly Shot Up."

"I never would have been able to do it if it hadn't been for Captain Barton, sir," said the copilot. "He talked me through it all the way back from Frankfurt. He never complained about his wounds. He's the real hero. You better go and look at him. I think he's been unconscious for the last few minutes."

The surgeon climbed into the plane and the crew gathered around, waiting for word on Brick's condition. After a moment the surgeon came out. He looked grim and color had drained from his face.

The surgeon took the copilot aside and asked him if he was sure about having talked to Captain Barton during the return flight.

"Of course I'm sure," said the young man. "I told you we would never have been able to make it back if it hadn't been for his help."

"That's impossible," said the ashen-faced flight surgeon. "Captain Barton was shot in the head. He died instantly, and he's been dead for nearly an hour."

Books by Daniel Cohen

BEVERLY HILLS, 90210: Meet the
    Stars of Today's Hottest TV Series
GOING FOR THE GOLD: Medal
    Hopefuls for Winter '92 (with Susan
    Cohen)
THE RESTLESS DEAD: Ghostly Tales
    from Around the World

Available from ARCHWAY Paperbacks

GHOSTLY TERRORS
THE GHOSTS OF WAR
PHANTOM ANIMALS
PHONE CALL FROM A GHOST:
    Strange Tales from Modern America
REAL GHOSTS
THE WORLD'S MOST FAMOUS
    GHOSTS

Available from MINSTREL Books

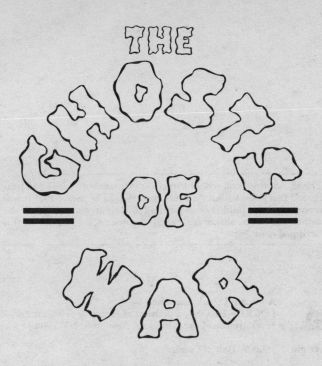

THE GHOSTS OF WAR

DANIEL COHEN

A
MINSTREL®
BOOK

PUBLISHED BY POCKET BOOKS

New York   London   Toronto   Sydney   Tokyo   Singapore

A Minstrel Book published by
POCKET BOOKS, a division of Simon & Schuster Inc.
1230 Avenue of the Americas, New York, NY 10020

Copyright © 1990 by Daniel Cohen

Published by arrangement with G. P. Putnam's Sons,
a division of the Putnam Publishing Group

All rights reserved, including the right to reproduce
this book or portions thereof in any form whatsoever.
For information address: G. P. Putnam's Sons, a division
of the Putnam Publishing Group, 200 Madison Avenue,
New York, NY 10016

ISBN 0-671-74086-5

First Minstrel Books printing January 1993

10 9 8 7 6 5 4 3

A MINSTREL BOOK and colophon are registered trademarks
of Simon & Schuster Inc.

Cover art by Lisa Falkenstern

Printed in the U.S.A.

For Hope

Contents

INTRODUCTION

The Reader is Warned (Again)

THOSE OF YOU who have read the introduction to some of my previous ghost books may already know what I'm going to say. But some of you must be new readers, or if you've read other books you haven't read the introduction, or if you did you don't remember what I said. So I'm going to repeat myself, because I think it's important.

A lot of people say to me, "Oh, you write ghost stories." Well, not exactly. These accounts are about ghosts, and I guess you could call them stories, and I did write them. But I don't really "write ghost stories." That statement implies that I make the tales up. I don't. I wish I did, because there are some pretty darn good ones here and I would like to take complete credit for them. I can't.

These are accounts that I have heard or read elsewhere. I simply collect them and retell them. I report them. I don't make them up.

The next question is usually "You mean these are all true?" That's a tricky one. These stories are always "told as true." That is, the teller either believes they are true or wants you to believe it. Some people, probably a lot of people, do believe they are true, or at least that some of them are.

To be quite honest, some of these accounts are pretty clearly not true. Or they concern things that happened so long ago, or the evidence is so slight, that there is not good reason to believe that they are true. In other cases, admittedly a smaller number, there has been some investigation to determine what really happened.

So, though I didn't make these tales up, somebody surely made up some of them. In other cases, an ordinary or explainable event is made to seem extraordinary, even supernatural, because of poor memory, overactive imagination, and the unconscious embellishment that comes with retelling an experience. And then there are those cases which, well, make you wonder.

In this book I'm not trying to prove or disprove anything. I am quite simply recounting for your entertainment some tales that people have believed. Take them for what they are, tales meant to make you shiver, and perhaps wonder. Remember the best ghost tales are always supposed to be true—even if they aren't.

All the accounts in this book are about ghosts that are in one way or another connected with war. There are haunted battlefields, soldiers' premonitions of death—that sort of thing. War has often inspired ghostly tales.

While accounts of ghostly events have been known throughout history and in all parts of the world, a large percentage of the incidents in this book come from World Wars I and II, and they come from England. Why? Quite simply because there are more World War I and II ghost accounts, and the English have been the most diligent people in the world in collecting ghostly tales. The Japanese are also great collectors and tellers of ghost stories, and there is a famous Japanese tale in this book.

I once discussed the prevalence of English ghosts with the great spirit medium Eileen Garrett. I met her after she retired and was living in a huge villa in the south of France. By the way, Eileen Garrett figures prominently in one of the tales in these pages. I asked the medium why there were so many ghost accounts from England, and relatively few from France or other countries in Europe. Were there more ghosts in England? Or did the English just talk about them more often? She thought about the questions for a moment. Then she said she didn't have the faintest idea. I don't either, that's just the way it is.

There are very few ghostly tales from either the Korean War or the war in Vietnam. Once again I have absolutely no idea why. I'm not trying to ignore these wars. It's just that the information isn't there.

Perhaps these wars, particularly Vietnam, are still too recent. It often takes many, many years before a ghost appears. Or before those who have encountered one are willing to talk about it. Maybe in another ten or twenty years there could be a whole bookful of Vietnam War ghost tales.

In the meantime there are enough strange accounts of wartime ghosts to engage your attention for a while.

And just remember. If you want to repeat one of these accounts for your friends, be sure and tell them it's absolutely true. You know it is because you read it in a book.

1

Haunted Battlefields

DO PLACES WHERE violent deaths took place somehow absorb the horror of the events? Can these impressions be released again like photographs printed from a negative? Some people believe that is what happens. That's why ghosts are reported most often at places where people have died by violence.

If this is the case, then battlefields should be prime places for hauntings. And so they have been. From ancient times startled observers have reported seeing the ghosts of long-dead warriors and soldiers repeating the battles in which they fell.

One of the best known of all the haunted battlefields is located just seven miles outside the English town of Banbury. It is a place called Edgehill. On October 12 of 1642 the first major battle of the English Civil War between supporters and opponents of King Charles I was fought at Edgehill. Four thousand men were said to have died in the slaughter. Neither side really won the battle.

That Christmas Eve some shepherds in the area swore that they saw two armies of phantoms battle one another on the field at Edgehill. It was a reenactment of the battle that had taken place there just a few months earlier.

The terrified shepherds told their minister. So the next night the minister and several other leading citizens stood on a hill overlooking the battlefield. They too reported seeing the same mass of ghostly soldiers, "with ensigns displayed, drums beating, muskets going off, cannons discharged and horses neighing. . . ." This group of solid and responsible observers said that the whole battle was repeated by the ghosts. The entire ghostly drama took over two hours; the length of the original battle at Edgehill.

After that people from all over the countryside gathered to witness this astounding spectacle. Within a few weeks, news of the ghostly event reached the ears of King Charles. He was so impressed that he sent six trusted officers, headed by Colonel Lewis Kirke, to investigate. The six visited the spot themselves. In their report to the king they said they had seen the ghostly battle with their own eyes. Some members of Kirke's group insisted that they actually recognized among the ghosts men they had known who had fallen at Edgehill. One of those mentioned was the king's standard-bearer, Sir Edmund Verney. The king was very much moved by what the officers told him.

This, by the way, was one of the first actual investigations of a report of ghosts. King Charles thought the ghostly battle was a good omen, that the rebellion against him would be put down. He was wrong. Six years later he lost his throne and his head.

After these first reports hardly a year passed without people telling of an appearance by the ghostly armies of Edgehill. Usually the sightings were reported on October 12, the day of the battle, or at Christmas.

During World War II the War Department fenced off the Edgehill area, and there were no more reports of ghosts. Though the area is now unfenced, there have been few reports of the ghostly armies in recent years.

Two years after the battle of Edgehill another major battle in the English Civil War was fought nearby. It was at a spot called Marston Moor. Edgehill ended in a draw. Marston Moor ended with a complete defeat for the supporters of Charles I.

From time to time people have reported seeing a full-scale ghostly reenactment of this battle. But these appearances have been nowhere near as celebrated as those at Edgehill. Still, there have been some very unusual experiences recorded at Marston Moor.

In November 1932 a couple of motorists were driving on the road that runs right though the old battlefield. Ahead of them they saw a group of four ragged men stumbling along. The motorists slowed down in order to get a good look at the group. The men were wearing the wide-brimmed hats with feathers that were typical of the royalist armies in the days of Charles I. At first the motorists thought the four must be actors from some touring company still wearing their costumes. They soon found out differently.

A bus was coming the other way down the road. The four figures appeared to stagger into the path of the vehicle. The bus driver must not have seen them, for he didn't even slow down. The bus seemed to go right through these four strangely dressed men.

The motorists who had been watching the figures were horrified. They stopped their car and searched the road. They were convinced they would find the bodies of the four men. They found nothing.

From time to time even today travelers report seeing a solitary figure on the old battlefield. Usually it is the figure of a royalist soldier, still trying to flee the battle fought centuries ago.

In the 1930s at least one English traveler reported seeing a ghostly reenactment of a battle that took place in 1689. The place was the Pass of Killiecrankie in the Highlands of Scotland. It was there that the Scottish Highlanders and other followers of James II defeated the English troops of William and Mary. The defeat of the English was complete. But it was the only major victory the Scots were able to muster. Ultimately, the more numerous and better-armed English forces completely overwhelmed the brave but outnumbered Highlanders.

The visitor had bicycled out to the pass to look at the old battle scene. The ride was a long and exhausting one and she fell asleep. When she awoke she saw a crowd of red-coated English soldiers fumbling with their guns. They were surprised by a horde of fierce Highland warriors carrying shields and brandishing swords. The visitor watched in horror as the British were slaughtered.

She then saw the image of a young Highland woman moving silently among the dead and dying British soldiers. The woman quickly and efficiently removed all the buttons and buckles and other items of value from the uniforms of the men. Any man who was still alive was stabbed with the broad-bladed dagger she carried.

The young woman was a scavenger. Such people often were found on battlefields during that era. Once the battle was over, the scavengers collected what they could.

The terrified observer actually fainted at the gruesome sight. When she awoke it was morning. The pass was quiet and deserted. Had she simply experienced a vivid nightmare? Or had she really seen a vision of that awful battle? The woman was convinced that what she had seen was much more than a dream.

A different sort of haunting afflicted some more modern Highland soldiers during World War II. In June 1940 a company of Scottish Highlanders was part of the British forces fighting the Germans outside Dunkirk in northern France. The British troops had been taking a terrible beating. The Scots, who were always in the forefront of the fighting, had suffered exceptional losses. Finally they were pinned down by German fire in a little wooded area.

Normally the Highlanders were the bravest of the brave. But once inside the wood they seemed to lose all their will to fight. The sergeant major of the Scots came to his commander,

Lieutenant John Scollay, and told him they had to get out of the wood at all costs because it was haunted.

Lieutenant Scollay was astounded. He didn't believe in ghosts. And he didn't think his men would be frightened of anything.

But the sergeant major was clearly frightened, and he wouldn't change his mind. "The wood is haunted, sir," he said. "I know it and the lads know it. For the love of God, sir, we're not scared of Germans. If we have to we'll advance, or force our way through the Germans. But we can't stay here another night."

Foolish as the idea sounded, Lieutenant Scollay saw that his brave men were beginning to lose their nerve.

"It's just a presence, sir," explained the soldier, "but we've all felt it. It's a kind of force pushing us away. And it's something that none of us can fight, sir—something uncanny."

Eventually the Highlanders joined the other British troops in retreat. Once out of the "haunted wood" Scollay's men regained their fighting spirit. But they could do nothing against the overwhelming odds. Most were either killed or taken prisoner.

Lieutenant Scollay himself was taken prisoner and spent the rest of the war in a German POW camp. He often thought about the "haunted wood."

When he was released after the war, Scollay did some research in the library at Dunkirk. He found that in the summer of 1415, a few months before the battle of Agincourt between the English and the French, there had been another battle fought in that very same "haunted wood."

Scollay wondered if the spirits of those long-dead soldiers had somehow come back to torment their successors some five hundred years later. Or was the area just so filled with an aura of death that the Scots were able to sense it? There had been no previous stories of that particular place being haunted. Did the modern violence release forces that had been quiet for five centuries? Scollay didn't know.

The British are certainly not the only people to have tales of haunted battlefields. Reports of phantom armies come from every land and every age. The earliest ones that we know of come from the Assyrians thousands of years ago.

According to legends, ghosts have been seen at the battlefield in Marathon, where in 490 B.C. the ancient Greeks dealt a crushing blow to the invading Persians. It was said that anyone who visited the battlefield after sunset heard the clash of steel, and the screams of the wounded and dying, and that they smelled the odor of blood. Anyone who actually saw the ghostly warriors was reportedly dead within a year. It was not a place people liked to visit at night.

2

The Samurai Ghosts

BETWEEN THE YEARS 1180 and 1185 there was a great war in Japan. It was fought between two powerful warrior clans, the Genji and the Heike. The two clans had been enemies for many years. They had often fought before. The Heike had usually come out on top. The emperor of Japan came from the Heike clan.

As with many wars, the reasons for this one seem unimportant to us today. What was important was that both clans were controlled by powerful warriors called samurai. The samurai were loyal and unbelievably brave. They would die rather than suffer defeat or disgrace. To the samurai, battle was the only way of settling differences. They did not believe in compromise.

And so, in May of 1180, the war, called the Gempei War, began. It was to become the most celebrated of all samurai wars, and the most deadly.

For years the war dragged on. First one side seemed to have an advantage, then the other. Finally it all came down to a single battle fought on April 24, 1185. Both sides had gathered all their forces near a place called Dan-no-ura. The battle is considered the most decisive samurai battle in all Japanese history.

The samurai, like the knights of the middle ages in Europe, were heavily armored warriors. They fought with swords and bows and arrows. They were not really sailors. Yet the battle of Dan-no-ura took place at sea. Japan is a series of islands. The armies needed simple boats to transport troops from one place to another. The boats had no armaments of their own. They were just floating platforms for the samurai. These were the boats used at Dan-no-ura.

As the battle began, the Heike seemed to be winning. Their archers took a grim toll of the Genji warriors. Then the tide in the ocean changed and the advantage shifted to the Genji. Very soon it became apparent that the Heike were going to suffer a humiliating defeat. They could do nothing to avoid the disaster.

The Heike commander then went aboard the vessel that was carrying the eight-year-old emperor. He announced that the battle was lost. In accordance with samurai tradition he said that suicide was the only answer.

The grandmother of the boy emperor took the child in her arms and walked slowly to the edge of the ship. She offered a prayer to her imperial ancestors and to the Buddha. Then, still clinging to the child, she jumped into the ocean.

That began the most tragic mass suicide in Japanese history. Practically every one of the Heike samurai drowned himself. So did all the members of the imperial court.

The red banners of the Heike floated on the sea and washed up on the shore. The beach was dyed a scarlet color. One commentator on the battle wrote:

"The deserted empty ships rocked mournfully on the waves, driven aimlessly hither and thither by the wind and tide."

The battle of Dan-no-ura marked the utter destruction of the clan that had once been the most powerful in Japan. The name of the Heike simply disappeared from Japanese history.

The sheer scale of the horror left a profound impression on the Japanese. The story was told and retold many ways throughout the centuries. Poems and songs were written about the battle and its aftermath. And it has become a central theme for many Japanese ghost stories.

For centuries sailors avoided the area of Dan-no-ura. They feared that they might catch sight of the restless ghosts of the Heike, who had been condemned to wander the area for eternity.

Peasants reported seeing ghostly armies bailing out the sea with bottomless dippers. It was said they were attempting to cleanse the sea of blood, a task that could never be accomplished.

The ghosts were supposed to try to sink ships, or pull down anyone foolish enough to swim in such a cursed area.

Other tales were told about the Oni-bi, or demon fires. On dark nights thousands of ghostly fires have been seen hovering about the beach at Dan-no-ura or flitting on the surface of the water. These are supposed to be restless spirits.

The wind at that spot has a peculiar sound, like the shouting of thousands of voices or the clamor of battle.

Most singular of all the legends surrounding this terrifying event is that of the crabs that inhabit the area. They are called Heike crabs. The shell of the crabs appears to bear the image of a human face. The crabs are supposed to contain the spirits of dead samurai.

In order to put the spirits to rest, a large Buddhist temple was built near the site of the battle. A cemetery was also built close to the beach. In it were monuments to the dead emperor, and all the principal members of his court.

These signs of respect are supposed to have quieted the restless spirits somewhat. They were not seen or heard as often after the temple and cemetery were built. Still, the spirits had not found perfect peace. Hundreds of years after the battle of Dan-no-ura, it was still considered foolhardy to wander the beach at night, particularly in late April, the time when the terrible battle took place. Then the ghosts would appear, and there was no telling what they might do.

3

The Angels of Mons

SOMETIMES WE WANT to believe something so badly that we do, even when there is overwhelming evidence that what we believe is not true.

Nothing in the long history of ghostly lore illustrates this better than the case that has been called The Angels of Mons.

When World War I began, many of the people of Britain were very enthusiastic about it. They thought that they would win quickly and easily; that the war would result in a great and glorious victory for Britain. Of course, the other side, the Germans, thought exactly the same thing. As it turned out, the war wasn't quick and easy for anyone. It went on for years and was much more horrible than people on either side had imagined. Hope for a quick victory soon gave way to fear and despair.

There was an early indication of just how long and terrible the conflict would be. The war began in August 1914. On August 23, British soldiers in Europe faced their first major battle. It was outside the city of Mons in Belgium. The British were hopelessly outnumbered. They had to retreat. The retreat was a long and hard one. They had to go as far as the Marne River in France before they could join up with French forces and launch a counteroffensive.

News of the retreat from Mons hit the British public hard. Those who had been saying the war would be short and glorious now realized that it would be neither. People in Britain became very depressed.

A newspaperman and writer of supernatural stories, Arthur Machen, wrote an imaginary account of the British retreat at Mons. He said that ghostly archers had joined the British troops during the retreat. Several famous battles had taken place near Mons hundreds of years earlier. Most assumed the phantom soldiers were English bowmen from the Battle of Agincourt in 1415. The English had won a great victory in that battle. The story implied that their troops had been given some sort of supernatural aid by ghosts from the past. It was a reassuring tale. But it was entirely made up. Machen had never really tried to pretend that the story was true.

Yet the British public was so hungry for good news that many seized upon Machen's tale as a factual account of what had happened. The story grew day by day. Soon people were saying that the British had been saved by a ghostly army of sword-wielding horsemen. Some said the phantom army appeared in the sky. Others insisted that "warrior angels" had actually been fighting alongside the British troops.

Popular songs were written about the "Angels of Mons."

All of this surprised, even shocked, Arthur Machen. He had never imagined that his little story would provoke such a reaction. He had not counted on people's will to believe, particularly under the strain of war.

Machen began telling people that his story was just that—a story—something he had made up. He wrote letters to newspapers confessing what he had done. But that wasn't what people wanted to hear. They got mad at him. They wrote him angry letters. How could he be so unpatriotic? they said. The Angels were on the side of the British.

Others began saying that they had heard about the ghostly figures before Machen wrote his story. Some said that the sightings had been confirmed by their son, or nephew, or brother who had actually been at Mons and seen them.

Later some Germans claimed that the images were motion pictures projected on the clouds by German pilots. This they said was an attempt by the Germans to make the British think that the angels were on the German side!

None of this was true. The whole story came completely out of Arthur Machen's imagination. All the rest was the result of people's strong will to believe. Even today you can find some references to the Angels of Mons as something that people really saw. But they didn't.

Perhaps people were more likely to believe in the Angels of

Mons because they had already heard stories and legends about phantom armies.

So when Machen wrote his story he knew there was an old belief in phantom armies. But he didn't believe in the Angels of Mons, and nobody else should have either. But they did.

4

The Polish Mercenary

A MEDIUM IS a person who is supposed to have a special ability to contact the spirits of the dead. A medium will go into a trance and then his or her body is taken over by the spirit. The spirit often speaks through the medium. Typically a medium has a spirit guide or control who introduces other spirits. In cases of hauntings or other ghostly events, mediums are often brought in to contact and identify the restless spirits, and sometimes to lay them to rest.

It must be pointed out that an awful lot of people are convinced that there is nothing but fraud and wishful thinking in the whole idea of mediums. Many mediums have been caught red-handed in fraud, and have admitted to it. Just because a medium says that there is a ghost doesn't mean that there is. Still, mediums figure very prominently in many, many ghostly tales. Here is one of them.

In the early 1940s a popular New York City newspaper columnist named Danton Walker bought a house north of the city. He wanted to use it for weekends and vacations.

The house was old, and parts of it had been built in the days before the American Revolution. Lots of repairs were needed. It was located in a part of New York State where many Revolutionary War battles had been fought. The headquarters of the American Revolutionary War general "Mad" Anthony Wayne once stood nearby. The bloody battle of Stony Point had been fought just a few miles away. The house itself may once have been used to store equipment or house soldiers, or it may actually have served as a prison. There were no definite records from the time. But the house had certainly been there during the Revolution, and since there weren't many houses in the area at that time, it is reasonable to assume that it was used for something during the war.

Walker had heard rumors that the place was "haunted" even before he bought it. But all old houses are supposed to be haunted, so he didn't pay much attention to such rumors. It wasn't until 1944, when the house had been fully restored, that Walker began to go there regularly. Then things began to happen.

There were the familiar ghostly footsteps, mostly the sound of heavy boots tramping around empty rooms. There were unexplained knocks at the door when no one was there. Objects would disappear from one place and turn up in another days or weeks later. People who came into the house were oppressed by the feeling that there was something "unearthly" about it. A lot of people didn't like to visit Walker's country house. Finally Walker himself felt he couldn't even sleep in the place. He had his bed moved to a small building behind the main house.

Now, Danton Walker had a long-standing interest in ghosts. He had often written about the ghostly experiences of famous people in his newspaper column. Yet he never did anything about the ghosts that seemed to be disturbing his own house.

Then, in 1952, rumors of Walker's haunted house reached Eileen Garrett, one of the most famous mediums in the world. She lived in New York City and had built a solid reputation as a respected and responsible medium. She even started an organization to study hauntings and other phenomena that might be considered psychic. The famous medium asked Walker if she could visit his haunted house, and naturally he agreed.

On a stormy day in November 1952, Eileen Garrett and a small group of investigators from her organization drove up to the columnist's house in the country. They had cameras that would take pictures in the dark, and tape recorders to pick up any strange sounds. But the main tool was Mrs. Garrett herself.

Unlike many mediums, Eileen Garrett didn't go in for elaborate rituals. She looked around the house, then marched straight into the living room and sat down in a comfortable chair. The tape recorder was switched on and the medium fell into a trance almost instantly.

As soon as she went into a trance, her East Indian "spirit control," Unvani, began speaking through her. The voice of Unvani said that he was going to allow another spirit, the spirit that was haunting the Walker house, to take control. Unvani warned, "Remember that you are dealing with a personality very young, very tired, who has been very much hurt in life."

The change from the dignified and calm Unvani to this new spirit was startling. Mrs. Garrett's eyes popped wide open and she stared straight ahead in terror. But it was obvious that she saw nothing. Her body started to tremble violently and she began moaning and weeping. The medium fell out of her chair and dragged herself across the floor to where Danton Walker was sitting. When she tried to stand up, her leg gave way as if it had been broken. She lay on the floor shaking and crying. It was several minutes before any of the startled people in the room could make contact with the spirit that was supposed to be controlling the medium's body. Even then they could get little information, for the spirit seemed to be confused, in great pain, and spoke very little English.

What those in the room could figure out from the garbled speech was that the spirit was that of a Polish mercenary named Andreas, who had served with the Revolutionary army. He had been carrying some sort of map when he was trapped by British soldiers in that very house. They beat him horribly and left him for dead. But he did not die at once. He lingered on for several terrible, pain-filled days. The Andreas spirit also mentioned a brother, but at first no one could make head or tail of this.

Unvani once again resumed control of Mrs. Garrett's body. She got up off the floor, bowed, and sat down in a chair.

Unvani's calm voice explained the situation further. He said that Danton Walker resembled the dead soldier's brother, another mercenary, who had also been killed during the Revolutionary War. When Walker purchased the house, and started coming regularly, the resemblance triggered the haunting by Andreas' restless ghost.

Unvani suggested that everyone pray for peace to finally come to the troubled spirit of the Polish mercenary. At that, Mrs. Garrett awoke from her trance. As usual she said that she had no idea of what had happened while she was under the control of the spirits. The whole experience had taken about an hour and fifteen minutes.

A few months later Walker reported that the atmosphere of his house seemed much calmer. Perhaps the spirit of the unhappy soldier finally did find its rest.

5

A Hero's Ghost

STEPHEN DECATUR was one of America's greatest naval heroes. Handsome, charming, and fiercely patriotic, he was idolized during the early 1800s. Decatur is the man who popularized the saying "My country right or wrong."

Decatur had come from a family of seafarers. He had served on a variety of ships throughout the Caribbean and the Mediterranean. In 1803 he was given command of his first ship. He carried out a daring raid against pirates in Tripoli harbor in North Africa.

During his career he had faced death many times. In one encounter he had seen his own brother fall dead at his side. In another his best friend had chosen to be blown up in a shipboard explosion rather than risk capture.

But the encounter that ultimately led to Stephen Decatur's early death was one that he had not personally taken part in. Though the United States had successfully defeated the British in the War of Independence, there were still many hostile encounters between the two nations. Most of these took place at sea. In one the British frigate *Leopard* fired at the American frigate *Chesapeake*. The American commander, James Barron, did not fight back. He allowed the British to board his ship and remove four sailors who they claimed were deserters.

When Barron returned to Norfolk, Virginia, he faced a court-martial for not resisting the British. One of those on the nine-member board was Stephen Decatur. Barron was convicted and suspended from the navy for five years. The *Chesapeake-Leopard* encounter was part of the slow-burning fuse that finally ignited the War of 1812 between America and Britain.

Barron was bitter over what had happened to him. He believed he had acted properly. Barron particularly blamed Decatur for his conviction. His hatred was doubtless fueled by the fact that Decatur was made commander of the *Chesapeake*, his old ship. During the War of 1812, Decatur, aboard the *Chesapeake*, performed more heroic exploits. He became a bigger hero than ever before. Forgotten and embittered, James Barron plotted revenge.

After the war Decatur and his beautiful and soft-spoken wife, Susan, moved into an elegant new house on Lafayette Street in Washington, D.C. The Commodore, as he was often called, became one of the most popular men in Washington. He could have entered politics, or any other field he wished, and success would have been assured.

But in truth, Stephen Decatur was not a satisfied or happy man. He had spent most of his lifetime fighting at sea. It was the world he knew, and the world he loved. But now there was no war, and no prospect of war. He confided to a friend that he was ashamed that he might have "to die in my bed."

James Barron's suspension from the navy had expired. But he was always passed over for the posts he wanted. His naval career was effectively at an end. He was convinced that Decatur was the real source of his troubles, so he mounted a campaign to provoke Decatur into a duel.

Dueling was illegal, though it went on anyway. When he was young, Decatur had fought several duels. Dueling had become less respectable; however, it was still excused in young men who were considered "hot-blooded." Decatur was now a mature man. He did not seem anxious to fight another duel. Barron knew this and was persistent. Finally Decatur was goaded into reluctantly accepting the challenge. He wrote, ". . . if we fight, it must be on your own seeking."

Decatur did not tell his wife about the upcoming duel. The night before it was to take place, there was a party at the Decatur home. The guests knew nothing. Stephen Decatur, who was normally sociable, was gloomy and distracted that evening. He left the festivities early and went into his bedroom. There he spent a long time just gazing out the window.

Decatur was certainly not afraid of facing death. He had risked his life too often to have any fear. He knew, however, that even if he won the duel, his reputation would suffer. Perhaps he also had a premonition of how the duel would turn out.

Before sunrise of March 14, 1820, the Commodore slipped out a back door of his house carrying a box containing his dueling pistols. He met his friend William Bainbridge, who was to act as his second. The pair rode to a field near the small Maryland town of Bladensburg. The place was a notorious dueling field. A brook that ran nearby had been christened Blood Run.

The duel was to be fought at a mere eight paces—murderously close. It was certainly to be a duel to the death. The men were told that they were to take aim and could fire after the count of one, but not after the count of three. Witnesses reported that two shots rang out as soon as the count of two was reached.

Barron immediately fell, wounded in the hip. Decatur stood for a moment, but only a moment. He dropped his smoking gun, clutched at his right side, and fell. He had been mortally wounded.

Decatur was taken back to his home in Washington. His wife, Susan, was so grief-stricken that she was unable to bring herself to see him before he died. Decatur's last words were "If it were in the cause of my country, it would be nothing." They expressed the futility of his death on the dueling field.

Despite the manner of his death, the country mourned its hero. Flags flew at half-staff, and towns all over the country were named after him.

The Commodore's ghost didn't show up for a year. Then

some of the household staff at the Decatur home reported seeing his spirit standing at the window of the room that had been his bedroom. The spirit was doing what Decatur himself had done the night before the fatal duel—staring out morosely.

Once that story got around, the window was ordered walled up. It didn't stop the sightings. People passing the house, which still stands on Lafayette Street, report that they have seen the semitransparent form of the naval hero at the walled-up window.

People who have lived in the house also report that sometimes, early in the morning, they have seen his ghostly form slipping out of the back door. The figure carries a black box under its arm. Decatur would have carried his dueling pistols in just such a box when he left his house on the fatal morning of March 14, 1820.

Susan Decatur never really recovered from her husband's death. She fled their Washington home. Many considered her grief to be excessive. But it is said that at times she still can be heard weeping in the Decatur house. Perhaps she has not recovered from her grief yet.

6

"Rescue My Body"

ONE OF THE LESSER-KNOWN wars in American history is the conflict between the United States and Britain called the War of 1812. The war was fought primarily in the East and at sea. But one of the little-known facts of this little-known war is that there were battles fought along the Canadian border, between English troops in Canada, and Americans to the south.

At least one of these battles has produced a tale of love, death, and a ghost.

In the Canadian village of Windsor, just across the border from Detroit, lived a girl named Marie McIntosh. She was admired by all the young men of Windsor. No one loved her more than a British officer, Lieutenant William Muir. Marie was inclined to return the lieutenant's affections. But the style of the day required that girls remain reserved and coy. They could not express their feelings or appear to give in too easily. Muir himself was reserved, often very nearly tongue-tied in her presence.

Lieutenant Muir's regiment was selected to attack an American force at a place called Mongaugon on August 12, 1812. His troops were to lead the attack. It was a very dangerous assignment. It was one from which there was a good chance that he would not return alive.

This threat spurred the lieutenant to unaccustomed boldness. The night before the scheduled attack he went to Marie to ask, to very nearly demand, her pledge of love and loyalty. Marie was taken aback. He had always been so shy. Now suddenly he insisted on complete devotion.

Her reply was curt. She told him she didn't know whether she would be his or not. "It remains to be seen whether I might not find another more to my liking. After all, the life of a soldier's wife is not the best for a respectable young woman."

The young lieutenant said nothing. He simply turned on his heel and left. Marie was startled. She had expected some discussion, some argument. After a moment she ran outside, but he had already mounted his horse and could not hear her calling after him.

"Men are so foolish!" she shouted. "If a woman does not immediately say yes, they feel wounded."

Marie slept fitfully that night. She was oppressed by a feeling of doom. The sound of footsteps in her room woke her.

41

She saw the figure of Lieutenant Muir staring down at her. His face was a ghastly white, and blood ran from a terrible wound on his forehead.

"Don't be afraid, Marie," the form said. "I died honorably in battle. But I beg only one favor of you. My body lies in a thicket. Rescue it from the forest and bury it in a respectable grave." The figure then reached out and touched Marie's right hand. She collapsed and did not awake until morning.

Had the ghost of Lieutenant Muir visited her in the night, or had she only dreamed it? Then she looked at her hand where the figure of the lieutenant had touched her. There was now a deep red mark embedded in her palm.

Marie dressed quickly, saddled her horse, and rode to the British headquarters. She told the commander, an old family friend, of her experience. He arranged to have her escorted across the river to the battlefield.

Marie found her lieutenant's body in a thicket, just as the figure had said. There was a bullet hole through his head. His body was carried back to the British camp, where it was buried with full military honors.

The ghost of Lieutenant Muir did not make just a single appearance. For many years people walking in the forest near Mongaugon reported seeing the lieutenant marching through the woods toward where the American forces would have been. His arm was raised, a saber held firmly in his grip.

Marie McIntosh eventually married an English nobleman. But she did not forget Lieutenant Muir. Each August 12, the anniversary of the battle, Marie would dress in black and go out in the street to beg for money to help feed the poor. She regarded this as an act of contrition for her thoughtless rejection of the lieutenant before his death.

Marie always wore a black glove on her right hand. Very few knew the reason for this curious habit.

7

The Guardsman's Terror

ON JANUARY 3, 1804, nineteen-year-old Welsh-born George Jones, a private in the Coldstream Guards, was on sentry duty at Recruit House in the center of London. (The place was later renamed Wellington Barracks.) Sentry duty was not one of the more pleasant assignments for a guardsman. He had to stand stiffly at attention inside his sentry box. Every fifteen minutes he had to march smartly out of his box for two hundred yards, until he met the other sentry coming from the opposite direction. Night or day, it didn't make any difference, the routine was the same. Officers often prowled the area. Any sentry not carrying out his duties exactly as set down in the regulations could be in serious trouble. No man at the barracks liked sentry duty. But none could avoid it either.

Sentry duty this particular night was unusually hard. It had snowed that day and the weather was extremely cold. Private Jones peered outside his box to make sure no officer was around. He then cradled his rifle in the crook of his left arm and rubbed his numbed hands together. The night was very quiet. The moon was full, and a silvery light shone on the trees in nearby St. James's Park. Despite the cold Private Jones felt oddly peaceful and contented.

The feeling of peace and contentment did not last for very long. As he looked out over the parade ground toward the canal, Private Jones saw a figure rise out of the earth not four feet away from him. It was the figure of a woman. The private could clearly see the make and pattern of her gown. It was made of cream satin with broad red stripes, and between the stripes were vertical rows of red spots. As the figure rose, it was surrounded by a glowing mist.

Jones was a brave man. Under normal circumstances he would have challenged the figure and called for aid from the other sentry. But there was something about this figure that absolutely froze him in terror and made him unable to move or to utter the slightest sound.

The woman had no head!

The stump of her neck stuck out of the lace-ruffled collar. The figure swayed a little, but made no attempt to move closer to Private Jones—much to his relief.

It must have stood there in front of him for fully two minutes. Then it turned and walked slowly and stiffly across the parade ground, toward the canal. When it had gone about fifty yards, it vanished.

At that moment Private Jones regained his voice and power of movement. Habit and training took over. Instead of running and screaming as most people would have done, he marched smartly out of his box to the halfway point between his box and that of the other sentry, Private David Rees.

"David, David," he called quietly. "Come here quick!"

Even speaking while on sentry duty was a breach of regulations. Rees was afraid an officer would hear them and they would both land in the guardhouse. "If you're fooling, George, I'll kill you," he said.

"I'm not fooling." Jones told him what had happened. Rees could tell that his fellow guardsman was not joking. He had been thoroughly terrified by something. But what? "It must have been a trick of the moonlight on the snow," Rees said sensibly.

Jones insisted it was no illusion. He knew what he had seen.

"You'll have to tell the sergeant of the guard, who is just coming up behind you," said Rees.

The sergeant of the guard couldn't image why his sentries were standing around talking that way. It was against all regulations.

"Private Jones says he's just seen a ghost, sir," said Rees.

The officer was not impressed. He wasn't any more impressed when he heard the private's story. "There are no ghosts in the Recruit House," the sergeant insisted. He told Jones to report to the guardhouse as soon as he was relieved.

As it happened, the officer in charge that evening was a

Welshman like Private Jones. He didn't particularly believe the young man's story. But he was not inclined to punish the Welsh private. He too had heard many ghost stories when he was a boy in Wales. He simply noted the incident:

"Private Jones, G., reported that while on sentry duty on No. 3 point, at about half after one in the morning, he saw the ghost of a headless woman on the parade ground."

He then sent Jones on his way and advised him not to see any more ghosts.

After Jones got some sleep, he thought about what had happened. In the cold light of day it all seemed too fantastic. He decided that Rees must have been right, it was the moonlight on the snow. In any case he wasn't going to say any more about it. Nor would Private Rees.

The whole incident would have been completely forgotten if it hadn't happened again three nights later. This time the sergeant of the guard found his sentry had fainted dead away in his box. When the man revived, he told of seeing the headless figure of a woman in a red-striped dress rise out of the ground just a few feet away from him.

A week later a veteran guardsman reported an identical experience.

Stories and rumors swept Recruit House. Things were beginning to get out of hand. The commanding officer of the base ordered an investigation. He hoped that this would put to rest all the rumors about headless ghosts.

Unfortunately for the commanding officer's hopes, the investigation turned up evidence that made the story more believable than ever. The investigators found that some twenty years earlier there had been a scandal attached to the Coldstream Guards at Recruit House.

A sergeant of the guards killed his wife. In a desperate attempt to make the corpse impossible to identify, he hacked off its head. The head was buried and never found, but the body was thrown in the canal near the barracks. That's where the ghost seemed to be going. The body soon floated to the surface. It was quickly identified because witnesses recognized the gown—of cream satin with red stripes and red spots between the stripes—that the body was clothed in. It was a dress that the sergeant's wife had owned.

No one could figure out a reason why the headless ghost suddenly decided to walk after twenty years. There was no record of the ghost ever having been seen before Private Jones reported it. And there seemed no way that Jones could have had any connection with the decades-old murder, or even know of it.

A clergyman was brought in. He spent a night in the sentry box, praying for the dead woman's soul. The ghost was never seen again. Just to be on the safe side, though, the sentry boxes at Recruit House were relocated so that none of them stood near the spot where the ghost had appeared.

8

Heard But Not Seen

IF THERE IS one characteristic common to all ghosts it's that they are elusive. They rarely appear on schedule in front of a large group of witnesses. They don't like to sit and have their picture taken. There have been a lot of "spirit photographs" since photography was first invented. But they are either so fuzzy and indistinct that they could be anything, or they are suspected, for very good reasons, of being frauds. For more than a century researchers and investigators have tried many methods of gathering solid scientific evidence of ghosts. These efforts have always fallen short. They may pick up some interesting bits of evidence, but no conclusive proof.

Some ghost hunters have used tape recorders. They have been able to pick up strange sounds that are difficult to explain. But they are not necessarily the sounds of ghosts.

In 1959 a man in Sweden gave the idea of recording ghostly sounds a new twist. He was recording the songs of birds in his garden. When he played the tape back he heard voices on the tape that he had not heard during the recording session. They were faint, difficult to interpret, but in his opinion very definitely there. So he tried recording under the same conditions again. He got the same results: strange and unexplainable voices when he played the tape.

These experiences started a worldwide interest in what has been called the Electronic Voice Phenomena or EVP. People from many different countries have reported picking up voices on tape that had not been heard during the recording session and should not be there. People who do this sort of thing often believe that the voices they hear are those of the dead.

It would be unfair not to point out that EVP is very controversial. Skeptics insist that what most people are hearing are really just scratches on the tape or some other sort of random noise. If the noises are amplified enough, or the speed at which the tapes are played is changed, then, with a considerable exercise of imagination as well, people can think that they are hearing voices. People once looked at photos where there was a blob of light or some other imperfection and thought they were seeing the faces of dead loved ones.

Imagination and wishful thinking are powerful influences on what we think we see, and think we hear.

Still, a lot of people do think that EVP means something. It has been tested in many places in the United States. One of the most interesting tests took place at a spot called Point Lookout.

Point Lookout State Park, in southern Maryland, is now a popular stop for tourists. During the Civil War, however, it was a scene of utter horror. Some say faint traces of this horror still linger.

The area was used by the government as a prisoner of war camp. It was officially known as Camp Hoffman. There were never any barracks. The prisoners lived in small tents. The land was low, marshy, and very unhealthy. There were regular outbreaks of smallpox, dysentery, scurvy, and other diseases. Between July 1863 and June 1865, over fifty thousand Confederate soldiers passed through the camp. Some four thousand of them died there.

Later some monuments to the Confederate dead were erected. In 1964 the land was purchased by the state of Maryland for a recreational area. It was then that the tales of strange and ghostly sounds began to circulate.

During the 1970s the park manager, Gerald Sword, lived in a large house on the park grounds. The building was called the Lighthouse. Sword swore the house was haunted. Doors opened and shut mysteriously; footsteps were heard in empty rooms and on deserted staircases. The sound of objects crashing to the ground would send people running to see what had happened. But nothing could be found.

Then Sword said he began hearing faint conversations. He could never pinpoint the source of the voices, nor could he hear what they were talking about. It was just the low and mysterious murmur of human voices. On other occasions he heard coughing and snoring. He felt invisible entities brush past him as he entered a room. And there was the constant feeling of being watched by unseen eyes.

Only once did Sword report actually seeing a ghost. He was sitting in the kitchen when he once again got that eerie feeling of being watched. He looked out the windows and saw the face of a young man wearing a floppy cap and a loose-fitting coat, looking back at him. He rushed to the window but the figure walked away and disappeared.

Sword thought that he could actually identify this particular ghost. It was not one of the Confederate prisoners. In 1878 a large steamer had broken up in a storm near Point Lookout. Thirty-one people were killed. The body of a young crewman named Joseph Haney was washed up on the beach at Point Lookout. He was buried near where his body had been found. Haney's description, printed in the newspapers of the time, matched exactly that of the young man Sword had seen at his window.

Another house on the property is located just across the road from the Confederate monument. It too has been troubled by strange and ghostly sounds.

A group of people interested in studying ghosts decided to try out the EVP procedure at Point Lookout. They figured that with so many reports of ghostly voices they had a chance at getting some on tape. Tape recorders were set up at places where the ghostly sounds had frequently been reported.

Though no voices were heard during the recording sessions, the group did believe they could detect faint voices and other sounds on their tapes when the tapes were replayed. One recording had what sounded exactly like the whistle of a steamboat. That would have been a common sound around Point Lookout many years ago, but steamboats have not operated in the area for a long time.

Men's voices on the tapes seem to use such phrases as "living in the Lighthouse" and "going home." Another interesting phrase heard on the tapes is "fire if they get too close." One woman's voice seemed to be using the word "vaccine" and another seemed to say, "Let us not take objections to what they are doing."

Do these tapes prove that there are ghosts at Point Lookout? They certainly do not. They are just another interesting bit of evidence about ghosts that has been collected. It's the sort of thing that keeps you wondering.

9

At the Moment of Death

PSYCHICAL RESEARCHERS—people who study ghosts and other strange events—speak of something they call a *crisis apparition*. A person sees the form of a relative or friend who should be hundreds or thousands of miles away. Then, after a few seconds, or a few minutes, the form disappears. Later the person learns that the individual he or she had seen had died, or was near death at the very moment the form appeared.

This is one of the most common forms of "ghost story." Thousands of these crisis apparitions have been recorded throughout history. They are particularly common in wartime, when men separated from their families often face sudden death.

Here are two examples from different wars.

Captain Eldrid Bowyer-Bower was a young British pilot. He was killed in action on March 19, 1917. That was during World War I. Three people in different parts of the world either saw him at the time he died or had some strong feeling that he had died. This happened long before they could possibly have known of his death by normal means.

The captain's half sister, a Mrs. Spearman, was in India when he died. She was sitting with her newborn baby on the morning of March 19 when:

"I had a great feeling I must turn around and did to see Eldrid. He looked so happy and had that mischievous look I had seen so often before. I was so glad to see him and told him I would just put the baby in a safer place, and then we could talk. 'Fancy coming all the way out here,' I said turning round again. I was just putting my arms out to give him a hug and a kiss but Eldrid was gone. I called and looked for him. I never saw him again."

At about the same time Captain Bowyer-Bower's niece in England, who was about three years old, also reported seeing him. Her mother described what happened:

"One morning while I was still in bed, about 9:15, she came into my room and said, 'Uncle Alley Boy is downstairs' (Alley Boy was a familiar pet name for the captain). I told her that he was in France, but she insisted that she had seen him. Later in the day I happened to be writing to my mother and mentioned this, not because I thought much about it, but to show that Betty still thought and spoke of her uncle of whom she was very fond. A few days afterwards we found that the date my brother was missing was the date on the letter."

The third experience did not involve an actual sighting. Just a feeling that something terrible had happened. The captain's mother received a letter from a Mrs. Watson, an elderly lady that she had known. Mrs. Watson had not written for almost two years. Then, quite unexpectedly, came a letter stating, "Something tells me you are having great anxiety about Eldrid. Will you let me know?" The letter was dated March 19, 1917, the day the captain was killed. At the time his mother did not know what had happened. Mrs. Watson later said that on the day she wrote she had an awful feeling the captain had been killed.

The second story comes from World War II.

Alexander Crockfield joined the navy just a few months before the attack on Pearl Harbor in 1941 that propelled the U.S. into the war. He took part in many of the early sea battles of the war in the Pacific.

His wife, Dorothy, had moved to California. She was expecting the couple's first child. Lieutenant Crockfield wrote regularly. He told his wife as much about what he was doing as the navy censors would allow. She knew that his ship was very active, and often in dangerous situations.

Mrs. Crockfield was naturally concerned about her husband's safety. But she was not overly concerned. Like many military wives she was able to keep from her mind the thought that anything could really happen to her husband. Tragedy might strike other people, but not her.

In due time the baby was born, a little girl, and Mrs. Crockfield filled her letters with details about the child. Her husband wrote back, eager for more information, even the smallest scrap. He also continued to be as informative as he could about what he was doing. His letters indicated that his ship was not in any unusually dangerous waters.

One evening she sat by herself rereading the latest letter from her husband. There was a noise in the child's room. Mrs. Crockfield immediately rushed to the door. Though the light in the room was dim, she could clearly see her husband standing by the baby's crib. He was wearing his tropical uniform and gazing down at the child.

Mrs. Crockfield tried to call out her husband's name. But before she could, the figure walked swiftly across the room and simply disappeared upon reaching the wall. A moment of joy gave way immediately to a sinking feeling of fear. It had not been her living husband in the room at all, but some sort of ghostly image.

When she went back to check on the infant, she noticed a pool of water near the crib, just where she had seen the figure standing. She dipped her finger in the pool and put it to her tongue. The water was salty. It was seawater. There was also something floating in the water, a piece of some sort of seaweed. She picked it up and carefully preserved it between two blotters.

A few days later the telegram from the Navy Department that Mrs. Crockfield had dreaded, yet expected, arrived. It informed her that her husband's ship had been sunk during a battle. He was missing and presumed dead.

When she had begun to recover from the shock, she took the bit of preserved seaweed to one of the large California universities. She found an expert on seaweed who was able to identify the curious and rare specimen. It was found only in the South Pacific, where her husband's ship had been lost. Legend had it that this particular type of seaweed grew only on dead bodies.

Not all crisis-apparition accounts involve a death. Sometimes, as the name implies, the apparition may appear when a person is in a grave crisis—possibly threatened with death. Would such an experience count as a "ghost story"? Most people think it does. Here is one, and you may judge for yourself.

In keeping with the theme, it is a military tale, and first appeared in a British army magazine called *Soldier*. It was written by James Simms.

On September 17, 1944, Simms, a British paratrooper, and others of his regiment were dropped into Holland. It was their task to capture a bridge in the center of a town called Arnhem. However, the Nazis had gotten information about the plan from a spy, and were waiting for them. The paratroopers were met with a deadly hail of gunfire. Many were killed, and most of the survivors, including Simms, were badly wounded.

The wounded were taken to a cellar in the town, where they had to stay for several days. Simms hovered between life and death. The men who were on either side of him in the cellar died from their wounds. But Simms hung on. He was finally shipped back to London, where he recovered.

When he was released from the hospital, Simms called a woman he had known since he was a boy. She told him that on September 19, while he lay nearly dead in that cellar in Arnhem, she had seen him. She had been sitting alone in her front parlor and suddenly had the feeling that someone was there. She looked up and saw the outline of Simms' figure. She accurately described how he looked at the time, right down to the thick bandages on his thigh. She said that he looked completely exhausted. He seemed to be holding on to the curtains on the window for support. It looked as if he were just about to step into the room. The woman had the feeling that something terrible was going to happen. She said out loud, "It's all right, Jim. It's all right." The figure then seemed to relax its grip on the curtains, and began to fade until it disappeared entirely.

According to Simms, the vision corresponded to the time that his condition took a turn for the better. On the 19th he had been very near death, but after that had begun to heal.

10

The Cursed Car

WARS RARELY START because of a single incident. Usually the tensions build up for a long time. There are a large number of potential points of conflict. Often different groups have different reasons for entering the same war. If the situation becomes bad enough, it may only take a spark to set off hostilities.

Nowhere in history can this be seen more clearly than in the start of World War I. The spark that set off that war was the assassination of the Archduke Francis Ferdinand of Austria by a young and fanatical Serbian nationalist. The assassination took place in the city of Sarajevo, in what is now Yugoslavia.

The war that exploded from this spark was fought primarily

between Germany on one side and France, Britain, and ultimately the United States on the other. Austria and the cause of Serbian nationalism played only a minor role in the war, which was responsible for some twenty million deaths.

But this is not a history book. This is a book about ghosts. Or in this case about how the aura of violent death may somehow be imprinted on an object so that others who come in contact with it may also be struck down.

In June of 1914 the Austrian Archduke and his wife were making what was supposed to be a goodwill tour throughout Central Europe, a region that was seething with unrest.

The royal couple arrived at Sarajevo, then capital of the state called Bosnia, on June 28, 1914. For his grand procession through the little city streets, Francis Ferdinand was given a blood-red, six-seat, open touring car. The car was impressive to look at, but provided absolutely no protection at all from potential assassins. The young fanatic, Gavrilo Princip, armed only with a small pistol, jumped out of the crowd, leaped onto the running board of the open car, and emptied his gun into the Archduke and Duchess, killing them both. Princip was captured immediately. He died in prison four years later.

Somehow the car survived the war. Afterward the newly appointed governor of Yugoslavia had the celebrated vehicle restored completely for his own use. However, after four accidents, one of which resulted in the loss of his right arm, the governor decided that the car was bad luck and should be destroyed.

However, the governor's friend, a Dr. Srikis, thought the idea of a cursed car was foolish. He bought the vehicle and drove it happily for six months. Then the overturned vehicle was found on the road. The doctor's crushed body was beneath it.

Another doctor bought the car. As soon as his patients heard about it they began to desert him. Perhaps they figured he wouldn't be around long enough to complete their treatment. Or perhaps they thought that the car's bad luck would rub off on them. Whatever the reason, the doctor's practice suffered greatly. So he sold the car to a Swiss racing driver. In a road race the driver clipped a stone wall, was thrown out of the car, and broke his neck. The car, however, needed only minor repairs.

The next owner was a wealthy farmer. The car stalled on him. Along with a friend, the farmer was towing it to a place where it could be repaired. Suddenly the stalled car started all by itself, killing both farmers.

Tiber Hirshfield, the car's next owner, decided it needed a new color scheme. Instead of blood red, he had it painted a neutral blue. Then, along with five friends, Hirshfield was driving to a wedding. There was an accident and four of the five were killed. The change of color hadn't helped a bit.

That ended the active life of the celebrated automobile. It was rebuilt and shipped off to a museum in Vienna, Austria. The car was so notorious that it attracted lots of visitors. The attendant in the museum, a man named Karl Brunner, used to regale visitors with stories of the "cursed" car.

In World War II bombs reduced the Vienna museum to rubble. No trace was found of the car. Or of Karl Brunner either.

11

Meeting in the Desert

CECIL BATHE WAS a Royal Air Force (RAF) mechanic. During World War II he was stationed in North Africa. He had driven a truckful of supplies from his base across the desert to another, about eighty miles away. He was returning to his home base when a sudden sandstorm blew up.

As the storm got worse, Bathe decided he had better wait it out. He knew such storms usually did not last long. He pulled his truck up alongside the wreck of a German tank that had been disabled in a battle about a month earlier. Hulks of this sort littered the desert after a battle.

Bathe didn't feel that he was in any real danger. The Germans had been decisively driven from the area. The storm would soon pass and he would be on his way again. He had a magazine with him, and a couple of bottles of beer that had been given to him by the Australian soldiers to whom he had delivered the supplies.

Bathe was sitting hunched inside his truck, reading and sipping his beer, when the whole vehicle seemed to be shaken by a strong gust of wind. He looked up and saw a lone uniformed figure standing amid the swirling dust and sand. Bathe opened the door to his truck and beckoned the man to come in quickly.

The stranger wore a ragged khaki uniform without any identifying insignia. He spoke English well enough, but with a rather strange clipped accent. None of this surprised Bathe. After two years of fighting in the desert, he was used to seeing men in ragged uniforms. As for the accent, well, there were a lot of different Allied troops fighting in North Africa. Bathe figured his companion might be Dutch, or perhaps a South African. He didn't know and didn't much care. Here was someone to share the loneliness of the wait in the desert with him.

Bathe gave the man a bottle of the beer the Australians had given him. The man accepted it eagerly. As he reached for the bottle, the Englishman noticed his companion had a large raw burn on his right hand and arm.

"That's a nasty burn," said Bathe. "You better have it attended to."

The man just laughed. "It's a bit late for that. Anyway, it doesn't matter." Bathe assumed that was simply a wounded soldier's show of bravery in the face of pain. He had seen that attitude many times before. He did not argue.

The two men chatted in an aimless sort of way. The stranger never gave his name or indicated where he had originally come from. But he did say that he had spent some time in England. When he was young he had been an enthusiastic Boy Scout, and he had attended an international scouting jamboree that was held in southern England. That bit of information caught Bathe's attention, for he too had been a Scout and had attended the very same jamboree. Perhaps they had met years before, Bathe said. "Perhaps we did," replied the man.

As night drew on, the sandstorm subsided. Bathe figured that it was time to make a run for his base. He wanted to get as far as he could before the desert became completely dark. The RAF man offered his visitor a lift, but the stranger shook his head. "I have to go in the other direction," he said. "But thanks for the beer."

The man stepped down from the truck and grasped Bathe's hand with surprising emotion. "God watch over you, fellow Scout," he said.

Bathe began to drive away, and glanced into the rearview mirror to see what the man was doing. He had disappeared. Bathe stopped his truck and got out to take a closer look. He could see nothing but the burned-out hulk of the German tank. The whole experience was an eerie one, and it troubled him all the way back to the camp. But he didn't dwell on what had happened. There was so much to be done that he quickly put the incident out of his mind.

Later in the week Bathe was making the same trip with his

supply truck. He passed the wrecked German tank again. Now there was a British salvage crew on the scene getting ready to haul it away. The wreck would be gutted for spare parts that might be of some use.

Bathe stopped to watch the salvage operation. The corporal in charge said that they had made a rather gruesome discovery. The driver of the tank had died at the controls a month before, when the tank had been hit by a shell. He was still inside the tank when the salvage crew arrived.

The body, which the corporal said had been pretty well preserved by the dry desert air, was laid out under a canvas next to the wreck.

A feeling of dread overcame Bathe. He didn't want to look under the canvas but knew he had to. The body was shrunken and partially decayed, but the features were quite clear. It was the same man he had shared a beer with a few days earlier. The burns on the dead man's hand and arm were clearly visible.

The corporal then said, "The strangest thing is that when we found the body there was a bottle of beer clutched in his hand. What's really strange, though, is that it was Australian beer. I wonder where a German tank driver got Australian beer."

Bathe said nothing. He just got back into his truck and drove away as quickly as he could.

12

A Visit to New York

DURING WORLD WAR II, a man named Oswald Remsen had a very strange experience. Later he never tired of telling his friends about it.

Remsen was a wealthy man. Every week or so he had to come into New York City on business. He had graduated from Harvard University. So when he was in the city he stayed at the Harvard Club, and he ate his meals there as well.

On this particular evening he was crossing Broadway at Forty-fifth Street near Times Square. In those days Times Square was still the heart of the theater district, not the sleazy dreadful place it became in later years.

Remsen had stopped to wait for the light to change before crossing the street. He was on his way to the Harvard Club, where he was going to have dinner alone. As he waited, two men in uniform stepped up next to him. He recognized the uniforms as those of the Royal Air Force, or RAF, from Britain. Remsen had seen RAF men in New York before. These two, however, appeared to be rather lost. They were looking around in wonder. They also seemed to be checking their watches against the large flashing sign on the New York Times Building.

One of the officers turned to Remsen and asked, "Is this Times Square?" Remsen found the question odd. Times Square was one of the best-known landmarks in the world. How could anyone not know he was in Times Square? Remsen assured the men that it was.

Remsen and the two Englishmen all seemed to be going in the same direction. They walked in silence for a few minutes. Then Remsen said a few friendly words. It was like a water faucet being opened. The two RAF men began chatting freely. They said they had never been in New York before, and they were full of questions. They commented on how exciting and alive the city felt after the grim restrictions that the war had imposed on England.

Remsen also recalled that every block or so one of the men would look at his watch. He wondered if they had an appointment of some sort. They said they didn't, that they were quite free for the evening.

"Then would you like to have supper with me at my club?" Remsen asked. The Englishmen seemed delighted at the suggestion. One of the men glanced at his watch and nodded to the other.

Dinner was excellent. The RAF pilots were lavish with their praise. They said they had not eaten so well since before the war. The three talked about the war, in a general sort of way. The two pilots, however, seemed unwilling to talk about their own experiences. Men at war often won't. Still, there was that annoying habit, as first one man and then the other looked at his watch.

"Are you sure you don't have an appointment?" Remsen said finally. "I don't want to keep you from anything important."

Once again the Englishmen assured the American that they were in no hurry to go anywhere. The conversation continued. They talked about the differences between England and America, and about the similarities. They talked about what the world would be like after the war. It was a pleasant and intelligent conversation.

Remsen had almost begun to ignore the men's habit of looking at their watches so often. Then, at five minutes to midnight, both of the men looked at their watches at once and rose from their chairs.

"Mr. Remsen," said one, "we would like to thank you very much. This has been a pleasant and unexpected evening. In many ways it's the strangest evening we have ever had."

That remark puzzled Remsen, and he said so.

"No, of course you don't understand," said the Englishman. "Let me explain. Just twenty-four hours ago, Bill and I were flying a mission over Berlin. We were shot down and killed. Now we have to be getting back. Thank you once again."

The two Englishmen started to walk toward the dining-room door and disappeared.

13

A Game of Billiards

BRITISH TROOPS WERE often quartered in large and stately old homes that the army had taken over temporarily. Many of the old houses in Britain are supposed to be haunted. Soldiers who stayed in them sometimes reported strange and ghostly encounters. None was stranger than that reported by Lieutenant Colonel Thomas O'Doneven.

In 1943 O'Doneven had taken some troops up to the Midlands—that is, the middle part of England—for training. They were staying in what he described as "a lovely old house, surrounded by parklands."

The owners had left the house. The only residents, aside

from the soldiers, were two old family servants. Colonel O'Doneven stressed to his men that they were guests in the house, not conquerors or invaders. They had to show respect for the property.

Dinner for the soldiers was at 7:45 P.M. each evening. One winter evening Colonel O'Doneven came down for dinner an hour early. He had not intended to be early. He speculated that he must have set his watch wrong. He looked at the hall clock and discovered his mistake. He decided that he would spend the hour sitting in front of the fire. Then he heard the sound of billiard balls clicking. The sound came from a room where O'Doneven had seen a billiard table. Being a keen billiard player himself, the colonel decided to investigate.

In the room the colonel saw a young man in uniform standing at the billiard table "knocking the balls about." He had never seen this particular fellow before, though he certainly should have remembered him. In the first place the uniform he wore looked strangely old-fashioned. Then the young man himself was bent over—slightly humpbacked. None of this seemed strange to O'Doneven. New men were always being moved in and out. He couldn't keep track of them, and didn't try. In 1943 the British were desperate for men. They might well have been taking people with handicaps into the army, particularly in noncombat jobs. As for the old-fashioned uniform, supplies were hard to come by, and perhaps that was the best they could come up with.

There was an hour to kill before dinner. Colonel O'Doneven asked the young man, "Want a game?" The man said nothing, but merely smiled agreeably. And so they began to play.

The game went on intensely and in total silence for nearly an hour. Both men were good and serious players. The score was tied. Then the colonel heard his officers moving around in the hall. He realized that it was almost time for dinner. He told his companion that this had to be his last shot. The young man nodded in agreement. The colonel took the shot—a good one that won him the game. "As I took my shot, he quietly put his cue back in the rack, gave me a smile and quietly walked through another door into what I afterwards discovered was a bathroom."

During dinner the colonel asked the other officers if they knew who his opponent at billiards had been. No one seemed to know him. "I was on the point of letting the matter drop, when I added, 'A nice lad, with a hump, I've just beaten him at billiards.'"

Upon hearing that, the old butler who was serving the dinner froze and went pale. "You've seen Master Willie, Sir," he said. The butler took a moment to recover, then he explained. "Master Willie" was the brother of the women who owned the house. He had joined the army during World War I. However, because of his deformity he was discharged and sent back home. "He came back here, Christmas 1916. He played a good game of billiards and shot himself in the room where he loved to play. We see him sometimes. . . ."

The colonel later told London reporter Dennis Bardens that during the game he had noticed nothing unusual. "It was all so natural," he said. "We just went on playing our shots as they came." They never spoke during the game. But Colonel O'Doneven said that he usually didn't speak while playing, and didn't like to be spoken to.

He reported that a couple of nights after the experience two of his junior officers saw the slightly humpbacked figure standing near a fireplace. Instead of checking more closely, they rushed upstairs to find some other officers as extra witnesses, and perhaps as extra courage. But when they got downstairs again, the figure was gone. However, the lights over the billiard table had been switched on.

After the war the house was sold to a new tenant. He dismissed the idea of ghosts. But Colonel O'Doneven recalled with some satisfaction that this new tenant did not remain in the house for very long. He sold it as quickly as he could, though he wouldn't say why.

14

The Haunted Air Base

ON THE SURFACE it was a simple enough assignment. A British film crew was going to make a management-training film. Much of the film was to be shot at a place called Bircham Newton in the county of Norfolk. Bircham Newton had been a Royal Air Force base during two world wars. More recently it had been turned into a school for students taking vocational courses.

The film project was to take only a few days. But from the start things began going wrong. Objects fell or were broken for no apparent reason. The scariest moment came when a heavy studio lamp nearly hit Peter Clark, a member of the film crew.

At the last second the lamp swerved, as if pulled away by an unseen force, and crashed harmlessly into a table. Clark had a narrow escape.

Just behind what was once the officers' dining room were indoor squash courts. Squash is a game very much like tennis. The courts had been built just before World War II and had been used by men at the air base. Another member of the film crew borrowed a tennis racket and a ball. He asked a few of his fellow workers if they wanted to have a game with him. No one seemed interested, so he went off to practice by himself.

There were two courts next to one another. The man from the film crew practiced first on one court, the one on the left. Then, for no apparent reason, he decided to switch to the other. As he began practice in the right court he heard footsteps behind him. At first he paid no attention. He simply assumed that another member of the film crew had come in to watch him. Then he realized that he had locked the door to the building when he came in. He was completely alone—or should have been.

For a moment he just kept hitting the ball off the wall. He didn't turn around. Then he heard a sigh. It was a sound that made him go cold all over. He turned around and saw a man wearing a World War II RAF uniform standing in the spectators' area. While he was watching, the figure vanished. That was enough for the film man. He ran from the building.

When he told his experience to Peter Clark, Clark had an idea. Why not go down to the squash court and try to record the sounds with the crew's tape recorder?

Later Clark explained, "It was a calm warm summer night

when we returned to the courts. We visited the left court, which felt completely normal. When we went to the court on the right, the atmosphere was so cold, so frightening, it was like stepping into another world."

The tape recorder was switched on and the men waited. But shortly an oppressive feeling made them so uncomfortable and fearful that they had to get out of the building. They locked the door and left the tape recorder running. By the time they came back the tape had run out.

When the tape was replayed it contained a lot of sounds that shouldn't have been there. There was the sound of aircraft and clanking machinery. These are sounds that would have been common during World War II, when Bircham Newton had been a working airfield. But such sounds had not been heard there for many years. Also on the tape was the murmur of voices, and what Clark interpreted as a strange and unearthly groaning. Both the tape and the machine were examined by an expert. There was nothing wrong with either one, nothing that could have accounted for the sounds.

Peter Clark had now become completely fascinated by the mystery. He got a group of his friends to go back to the old air base accompanied by a spirit medium. The aim was to find out what spirits were haunting the place. The medium identified the spirit of an airman called Wiley. As Clark continued to investigate the case he discovered that there had indeed been an airman called Wiley at the base during the war. He had committed suicide there.

As public interest in the haunting of Bircham Newton grew, others stepped forward with their tales. Some who had been students at the place after it had been turned into a school reported experiences common to many hauntings. They told of how the covers were torn off their beds at night, or how the curtains in their rooms were pulled down by an invisible force. There were those who said that unseen figures brushed past them or actually tapped them on the shoulder. One man claimed that he had seen a figure in an RAF uniform walk through a solid wall. He was so frightened that he dropped out of the school and left the very next day.

Finally the British Broadcasting Corporation (BBC) became interested. The BBC decided to do a special program on the haunting of the old air base. Two of Britain's leading spirit mediums were hired to help with the show. The mediums claimed that they knew little of the details of the case beforehand.

The mediums examined the squash courts. The left-hand one was normal. The right-hand court, however, held a "presence" according to the mediums. It was the spirit of a dead airman.

One of the mediums, John Sutton, fell into a trance. He began to speak in a different voice. His body had apparently been taken over by the spirit of a dead man. The spirit identified himself as Dusty Miller. He said he was a World War II airman who had been killed in a crash near the base along with two of his friends, Pat Sullivan and Gerry Arnold.

The spirit said that the three men had all been enthusiastic squash players, and that they had often used the courts on the base. They made a pact that if anything happened to them they would try to meet up again on the squash court where they had spent so many pleasant hours.

Shortly after making the pact the men were all killed during a training flight near the base. Now their spirits returned to the squash court just as they had promised.

The medium said that after the dead airman's spirit had been contacted, thus allowing the story to be told, the ghosts should finally be laid to rest. In fact, no more strange disturbances have been reported at Bircham Newton.

15

Return Flight

A LOT OF American pilots flew missions out of bases in England in World War II. One of them was an upstate New York man, Captain Charles "Brick" Barton.

Captain Barton was the pilot of one of the B-24s that carried out bombing missions over Germany during the spring of 1943. These missions were extremely dangerous. Many planes were lost to German antiaircraft guns and enemy fighter planes. Despite the dangers, morale among the American fliers remained high. Captain Barton himself was an incurable optimist. His good nature, supreme confidence, and great skill made him a real favorite with the others in his crew.

Though Brick himself had never been hurt, his plane had been hit several different times. His veteran copilot suffered an injury and had to be hospitalized. So when Barton's B-24 took off again, his backup was a young lieutenant on his first combat mission. And it was a tough one. They were to drop their bombs on the German city of Frankfurt, a well-defended target.

Though enemy fire was heavy, Barton's plane made it to Frankfurt, dropped its bombs on the assigned target, turned, and headed for home. But just a few minutes into the return trip, machine-gun fire from a German pursuit plane shattered the plastic glass of the cockpit. Brick was hit, his blood splattered over the instrument panel and around the cabin. Another burst of machine-gun fire ripped into the B-24's controls. The plane was flyable—but difficult to handle.

Brick said he was unable to fly the plane himself. His inexperienced copilot was forced to take over the controls. The young lieutenant very nearly panicked. Then he heard Brick's reassuring voice telling him what to do. Clearly the captain was badly hurt, yet he refused to be taken into the back of the plane where he might be able to lie down and be more comfortable. He remained in his seat talking calmly and quietly to his young companion. The copilot marveled at how clear Brick's mind was for a man who had obviously been seriously wounded and must have been in great pain.

The weather grew worse. The plane responded more and more uncertainly to the copilot's touch. Brick kept giving him helpful suggestions drawn from the experience of more than twenty missions over Germany. For nearly an hour the young copilot and the wounded veteran kept the plane on course back to its base in England.

As they neared base the copilot radioed for an ambulance. Brick had suddenly become silent for the first time during the return flight. The lieutenant worried that perhaps he had become unconscious from loss of blood.

The young man brought the balky and battered plane down to a safe landing and quickly climbed out to look for medical help. He almost bumped into the flight surgeon, who was running toward him.

"Good job bringing that plane in, young man," said the surgeon. "It looks to be pretty badly shot up. It couldn't have been easy to fly all the way back from Germany in that condition."

"I never would have been able to do it if it hadn't been for Captain Barton, sir," said the copilot. "He talked me through it all the way back from Frankfurt. He never complained about his wounds. He's the real hero. You better go and look at him. I think he's been unconscious for the last few minutes."

The surgeon climbed into the plane and the crew gathered around, waiting for word on Brick's condition. It didn't take long. After a moment the surgeon came out. He looked grim and color had drained from his face.

"Men, I'm afraid there is nothing I can do for your captain. He's dead."

The surgeon then took the copilot aside and asked him if he was sure about having talked to Captain Barton during the return flight.

"Of course I'm sure," said the young man. "I told you we

never would have been able to make it back if it hadn't been for his help."

"That's impossible," said the ashen-faced flight surgeon. "Captain Barton was shot in the head. He died instantly, and he's been dead for nearly an hour."

16

To Clear His Name

GHOSTLY LEGENDS OFTEN speak of the return of a spirit to correct some injustice. Perhaps to clear the dead man's name. That certainly seems to have been the case with Lieutenant Desmond Arthur.

On May 27, 1913, a little over a year before the start of World War I, Lieutenant Arthur was killed in the crash of his plane over the Scottish airbase of Montrose. Airplanes of that era were still crudely built and usually dangerous to fly. Lieutenant Arthur was piloting a BE2 biplane—that is a plane with a double wing. It seemed like a routine flight. He was gliding down from four thousand feet when one wing simply folded up in midair. The plane plummeted to the ground. Lieutenant Arthur was thrown out of the cockpit to his death. There were no parachutes in 1913.

A group called the Royal Aero Club investigated the accident. The conclusion these investigations reached was that somebody had botched a repair job. Just before Lieutenant Arthur's fatal flight a wing of the plane had been broken near the tip. The break had been repaired with a crude splice, and to conceal the shoddy work the man who did it put new fabric over the area. The repair looked all right but could not stand up to the stress of flight. That was the reason for the fatal accident. Lieutenant Arthur's friends said this carelessness amounted to murder. The guilty party, however, could not be identified.

In 1916 the war was on. There had been a number of fatal accidents to British planes. One member of parliament accused the government of doing nothing while men were "murdered . . . by the carelessness, incompetence, or ignorance of their senior officers or of the technical side of the service." It was a strong and very disturbing charge. One of the cases he cited was that of Lieutenant Arthur.

The government, however, was anxious to avoid any hint of scandal in the air service. They did not want public faith in the competence of those running the war effort undermined. So on August 3, 1916, the British Government issued its own report on the death of Lieutenant Arthur. The report said that the botched wing repair explanation that had been put forth by the Royal Aero Club was not correct. The obvious conclusion, said the government, was that Lieutenant Arthur had only himself to blame for his death. That conclusion enraged Arthur's friends, and may have enraged the dead man as well.

About a month after the government report was issued, strange things began happening at Montrose air base. One officer said that he was followed by a man in full flying gear. When he tried to get close to the mysterious pilot the figure vanished. A flying instructor woke up one night to find a strange man, again wearing full flying gear, sitting beside the fireplace in his bedroom. When the instructor challenged the intruder, he suddenly discovered that the chair was empty. Others in the base woke up with the unshakable feeling that someone else was in their room. But no one could be seen.

Stories of the strange occurrences at Montrose began to circulate around other air bases in Britain. Inevitably the name of Lieutenant Arthur was brought up. Was he the ghostly figure? Was he trying to encourage his pilot friends to help clear his name?

The stories also seemed to have some effect on members of the government commission who had issued the report blaming the lieutenant for his own death. A couple of them admitted publicly that they had never really studied the evidence. An engineer and a lawyer were called in to review the findings. Finally at Christmastime a new report was issued on the death of Lieutenant Desmond Arthur.

The report declared, "It appears probable that the machine had been damaged accidentally, and that the man (or men) responsible for the damage had repaired it as best he (or they) could to evade detection and punishment."

The guilty party remained unknown, but that conclusion

seems to have satisfied the restless spirit of Lieutenant Desmond Arthur. It made one more brief appearance in January of 1917—and was seen no more.

17

A Ghost of Yourself

IN EUROPE, particularly in Germany, there is a strong belief in what is called the doppelgänger, or "double." A person suddenly encounters a ghostly image of him or her self.

Probably the most famous account of the doppelgänger comes from the great German writer Johann von Goethe.

"I rode on horseback over the footpath to Drusenheim, when one of the strangest experiences befell me. . . . I saw myself on horseback coming toward me on the same path dressed in a suit as I had never worn, pale gray with some gold. As soon as I had shaken myself out of this reverie the form vanished. It is strange, however, that I found myself returning on the same path eight years afterward . . . and that I wore the suit I had dreamt of, and not by design but chance."

Goethe's doppelgänger experience was a simple one. Most often the doppelgänger is associated with impending death or illness or appears to be a warning.

One of the most extraordinary doppelgänger accounts comes from an American, Alex B. Griffith.

In the summer of 1944, during World War II, Griffith was an infantry sergeant, leading a patrol in France. Part of the country through which Sergeant Griffith and his men passed was said to be filled with German troops who were well dug in and waiting to ambush the Americans. But Sergeant Griffith's men had been on patrol for several days and saw no signs of the enemy. As a result they felt quite relaxed. They had begun to believe that the stories of the dangers had been exaggerated.

Still, Sergeant Griffith and his men remained alert as they walked down the road. Suddenly the sergeant was startled to see a figure on the road ahead. The man was wearing the uniform of an American soldier, just like his own. As Griffith looked more closely he realized there was more than a similarity in uniform. The man in the road looked just like him. It was his double. Though Griffith did not know the word, it was his doppelgänger. The figure was waving its arms frantically. It was also moving its mouth as if it were shouting, but Griffith could hear nothing. While Griffith couldn't hear what his double was shouting, none of the other men in the patrol seemed to see it at all. Yet it was obvious to Sergeant Griffith that the figure in the road was signaling him to stop.

His men were quite surprised when Sergeant Griffith suddenly told them to halt and turn around. He couldn't tell them why he wanted them to stop. All he knew was that if they continued along the road they would be in great danger. He had been warned.

Griffith told his men to rest for a few minutes. As he sat on the ground trying to figure out what to do next, an American jeep filled with supplies passed the foot soldiers and headed down the road to the spot where the doppelgänger had given its warning. There was a sudden burst of machine-gun fire. The jeep went wildly out of control, for the driver had been shot. Somewhere up ahead was a hidden German machine-gun emplacement that had been set up to guard the road. If Griffith and his men had gone any farther, they would certainly have been gunned down. Griffith's vision of his double's waving and shouting in the road had saved their lives.

Some twenty years later Griffith experienced a replay of this lifesaving vision.

The war had long been over. Griffith, no longer a sergeant but a civilian, was out on a hike in the forest with his family. There had been a tremendous storm the previous night. On this day the rain had stopped, but the winds were still gusty.

While walking down the trail, Griffith saw his double again. But it was not the Alex Griffith of 1964. It was Sergeant Griffith. It was the same uniformed figure he had seen in France. And, as in the previous vision, the figure was waving its arms and moving its mouth as if shouting a warning.

No one else saw the figure. But Griffith had not forgotten what had happened in France. He immediately had his family stop and turn back down the trail. A few seconds later a huge tree, weakened by the storm, came crashing down into the clearing where Griffith and his family would have been had they not stopped.

Once again the doppelgänger provided a lifesaving warning.

18

Commander Potter's Vision

THE LIFE OF a combat pilot is always in danger. In World War II among the most dangerous missions were those flown by British pilots who were stationed in Egypt.

Bombers from Egypt flew out over the Mediterranean Sea to drop torpedoes and mines in the path of German ships bringing supplies to General Erwin Rommel's North African troops. The missions were too dangerous to fly during the day because the bombers had to fly low and close to their targets. There was a constant risk of being shot down, either by the German ships themselves or by German planes protecting the supply ships. So the British bombers usually flew at night.

The best time for them was during a full moon, so that they could use the moon's bright reflection off the water as an aid to navigation. Such periods of full moon were called a "bomber's moon."

A dramatic and eerie tale was told by Commander George Potter of the RAF. He was a squadron leader at the RAF base in Egypt.

Since the missions were so dangerous, the periods between them were very tense. The men often tried to overcome their anxiety and fear with an air of forced gaiety.

One evening just before a bomber's moon, Commander Potter and another officer named Reg Lamb were in the officers' mess having a drink. Also in the room at that time was a wing commander whom Potter identified only as Roy. Roy was sitting with a group of his friends, and as Potter and Lamb finished their drinks and got ready to leave, there was a burst of laughter from the group around Roy. The sudden noise caused Potter to look in their direction.

It was at that moment that Potter had a strange and terrifying vision. "I turned and saw the head and shoulders of the wing commander moving ever so slowly in a bottomless depth of blue-blackness. His lips were drawn back from his teeth in a dreadful grin; he had eye sockets but no eyes; the remaining flesh of his face was dully blotched in greenish purplish shadows, with shreds peeling off near his left ear.

"I gasped. It seemed that my heart had swollen and stopped. I experienced all the storybook sensations of utter horror. The hair on my temples and the back of my neck felt like wire, icy sweat trickled down my spine and I trembled slightly all over. I was vaguely aware of faces nearby, but the horrible death mask dominated the lot."

Potter had no idea how long the ghastly vision lasted. Finally he became aware of Lamb tugging at his sleeve and saying, "What's the matter: You've gone white as a sheet . . . as if you've seen a ghost."

"I have seen a ghost," said Potter. "Roy, Roy has the mark of death on him."

Lamb looked over to where Roy and his friends were sitting. He saw nothing unusual. Potter was still white faced and shaking all over. Both officers knew that Roy was scheduled to be flying the next night. Neither man knew what to do about it.

In the end Commander Potter decided to do nothing. He first thought of going to the group captain with the story and asking that Roy be taken off the mission. But he knew that Roy would certainly have objected and would have refused to be kept from his crew for such a reason. And if Roy said he wanted to go, the request to have him grounded would undoubtedly have been denied.

Potter came to believe that his final decision not to try to do anything was the right one. It was, he said, part of "a predetermined series of events." Besides, in reality there was nothing he could have done.

The following night Potter was extremely nervous and tense. He was expecting the worst. Finally he got the message that he had been fearing. Roy and his crew had been shot down and forced to ditch in the ocean. But the ditching apparently had gone well. Another plane in the squadron had seen the men in the water climbing into a life raft.

Potter was relieved for the moment. He convinced himself that the men would soon be rescued and that his vision had been a false or misleading one. But as the hours dragged on, no sign of Roy and his crew could be found.

"And then I knew what I had seen," said Potter. "The blue-black nothingness was the Mediterranean at night and he was floating somewhere in it dead, with just his head and shoulders held up by his life preserver."

About the Author

DANIEL COHEN is the author of over a hundred books for both young readers and adults, and he is a former managing editor of *Science Digest* magazine. His titles include *Going for the Gold: Medal Hopefuls for Winter '92* (co-authored with Susan Cohen), *Beverly Hills 90210: Meet the Stars of Today's Hottest TV Series,* and *The Restless Dead: Ghostly Tales from Around the World,* all of which are available in Archway Paperback editions. His Minstrel titles include *The Ghosts of War, Real Ghosts, Ghostly Terrors, The World's Most Famous Ghosts,* and *Phone Call from a Ghost.*

Mr. Cohen was born in Chicago and has a degree in journalism from the University of Illinois. He has lectured at colleges and universities throughout the country. Mr. Cohen lives with his wife in New York.